The Great Shark Adventure

 S0-BRP-623

By MARY MĀDEN

Illustrated by Stephanie Kiker Geib

#1 in the **Earth/Ocean Adventures** series

© 1999 by Mary Māden. All rights reserved.
ISBN 1-890479-60-8
Published in the USA by DOG AND PONY PUBLISHING
P.O. Box 3540, Kill Devil Hills, NC 27948
Phone: 252-261-6905

Jamie looked all around him. He was in a strange and wonderful new world. Above and below him was clear, blue water.
He was scuba diving under the ocean!
Jamie could barely believe his eyes.

Everywhere he turned there was something different. The water was full of life! There were jelly fishes and squids pushing through the water. There were fish everywhere! Jamie hoped he would see some sharks. Jamie wasn't afraid of sharks — he loved sharks! He thought they were about the neatest things in the world.
Suddenly, Jamie saw something swimming ahead of him. Could it be . . . Yes! It was a shark!

The shark came closer.
Jamie could see that it
was a Tiger Shark.
And a big one at that!

Jamie wasn't really scared, but he stayed out of its way! Jamie knew that most sharks don't attack people . . . but, it is best not to bother a Tiger Shark. It will eat anything! Slowly the Tiger glided past. Jamie watched as the big, strong fish swam away. "Cool!" Jamie said to himself.

Jamie looked all around. Below him, Jamie spotted some Nurse Sharks. They lay on the sandy bottom, not moving.

"Wow!" Jamie cried, bubbles exploding from his breather. "There must be fifteen or twenty of them!" Jamie swam down to take a closer look.

Some of the Nurse Sharks had remoras on them. Remoras are little fish. They tag along on the shark and eat the pests that live on its body.

"I guess you're not afraid of sharks either," Jamie said to one of the remoras.

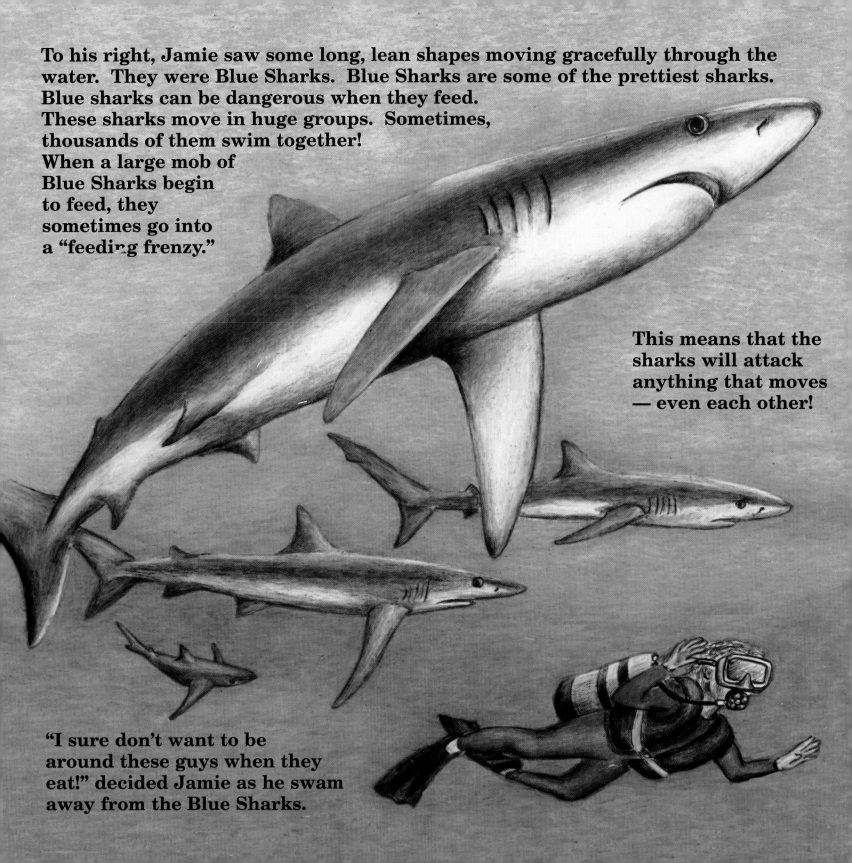

To his right, Jamie saw some long, lean shapes moving gracefully through the water. They were Blue Sharks. Blue Sharks are some of the prettiest sharks. Blue sharks can be dangerous when they feed. These sharks move in huge groups. Sometimes, thousands of them swim together! When a large mob of Blue Sharks begin to feed, they sometimes go into a "feeding frenzy."

This means that the sharks will attack anything that moves — even each other!

"I sure don't want to be around these guys when they eat!" decided Jamie as he swam away from the Blue Sharks.

To his left, Jamie saw something move. It was a large Bull Shark! It was hunting for food. Jamie knew that Bull Sharks are blamed for most attacks on people along coastal beaches. Jamie played it safe and kept his distance.

The Bull Shark spotted its prey — a smaller Dogfish Shark. The Bull Shark circled the Dogfish Shark. Round and round it went. Next, the big shark bumped the smaller shark. Finally, the Bull Shark came straight for the Dogfish Shark. With its sharp teeth, the Bull Shark took a bite.

Chomp!
Chomp!
Chomp!

The Bull Shark ate the small shark in three big bites!

Jamie swam on. Ahead of him, swam another big shark.

This one had a head shaped like a hammer. The Great Hammerhead Shark was swinging its head from side to side as it swam looking for its favorite food — stingrays. "Awesome!" said Jamie.

Suddenly, a huge manta ray jumped out of the water. It made a huge splash! "Wow!" cried Jamie, excited. Jamie liked rays almost as much as sharks. (After all, rays are close relatives to sharks!)

Jamie moved farther out in the ocean.
Here, a long way from shore, sport fish like tuna
swim the surface of the water.

Just then, a short fin Mako raced through the water.
The shark was chasing a swordfish. The Mako is the fastest
of all sharks. They can swim 40 miles an hour!
The Mako can leap 20 feet out of the water too.
"I hope that swordfish is a fast swimmer!" said Jamie
watching the two fish as they sped away.

Suddenly, Jamie saw a huge monster! The monster was as big as a bus. It was at least 45 feet long! It came straight for him. Its big mouth was wide open. Four people could easily fit into that enormous mouth. It could swallow Jamie whole in one gulp!

Jamie was nervous. The giant monster closed its mouth. Jamie breathed a sigh of relief! Not because the big monster closed its mouth, but because Jamie knew what the monster was. It was a Whale Shark! Whale Sharks are gentle creatures. They aren't whales at all. They are just named that because they are as big as a whale.

"Hi there, Big Girl!" said Jamie, coming close to the shark. "Nice girl!" Jamie reached out and petted the huge shark. Her skin felt like very, very rough sandpaper. The Whale Shark was the color of an elephant and had great, big polka-dots on it.

"How about a ride?" Jamie said, grabbing hold of the shark. He pulled himself onto its back and held on tight. Jamie was riding the biggest shark in the world!

The Whale Shark swam with Jamie on her back. She swam faster and faster. Jamie was having trouble holding on. He slid down the shark's back and tried to hold on to her tail. The tail swooshed from side to side. Jamie fell off.   A strong slap of the tail sent him tumbling!

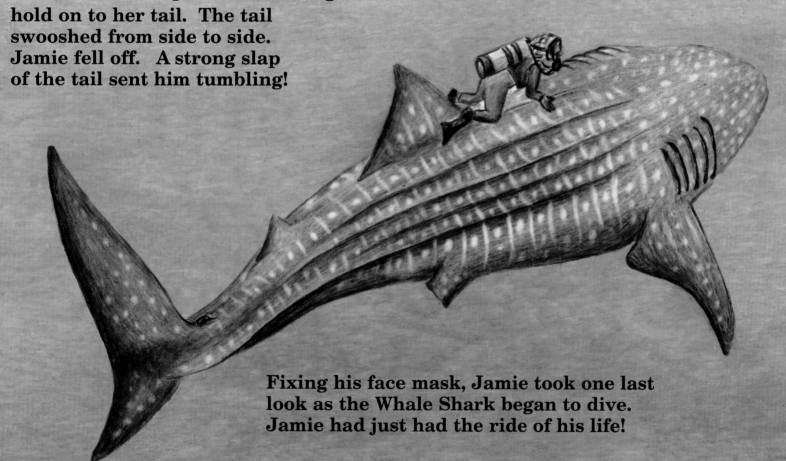

Fixing his face mask, Jamie took one last
look as the Whale Shark began to dive.
Jamie had just had the ride of his life!

Jamie turned around and headed back. He couldn't believe all the sharks he had seen! Suddenly, Jamie saw a shape move towards him. Out of nowhere appeared a White Shark or "Great White" as they are called. Jamie heard that the White Shark has no fear of man and may attack. Quickly, Jamie tried to swim away. The fierce shark headed straight for him! Jamie couldn't move. Then Jamie heard a strange sound. Ring! Ring! The shark came closer. The sound grew louder and louder. Ring! Ring! Ring! The big shark came closer and closer and closer until . . .

"Jamie!" called a familiar voice. "Jamie!"
Jamie struggled to swim to the surface.
Up and up Jamie came until he was out of
the deep blue world of sleep.

Jamie opened his eyes. He was in his bed. Jamie turned off the alarm clock. He sighed. It was a dream! His wonderful adventure had just been a dream!

Jamie's father came into the room. "Get up sleepyhead! I have to go!"
"I know. Dad . . .," the words tumbled out of Jamie's mouth. "Why can't I go with you? I can dive. You said so yourself that I'm good. I won't get in the way. Pleease!"
"Now Jamie, we've talked about this. A charter won't allow you to dive. You aren't old enough. Maybe next year when you get your junior certification, you can go. We'll see then."
"But, I know how to dive now!" interrupted Jamie. "Why can't I go now!"
"That's enough," said Jamie's dad. "Subject's closed! I'll be back in a few days. Be good and don't give Mrs. Johnson any trouble!"
"Sure Dad," said Jamie "... see you."
"Hey!" said Jamie's dad. "You forgot something."

"Aw, Dad!" complained Jamie as his dad gave him a hug.
"I'll miss you," Jamie's dad called out as he left, "... love you!"

"I am old enough to dive," mumbled Jamie. "I'll prove it!"

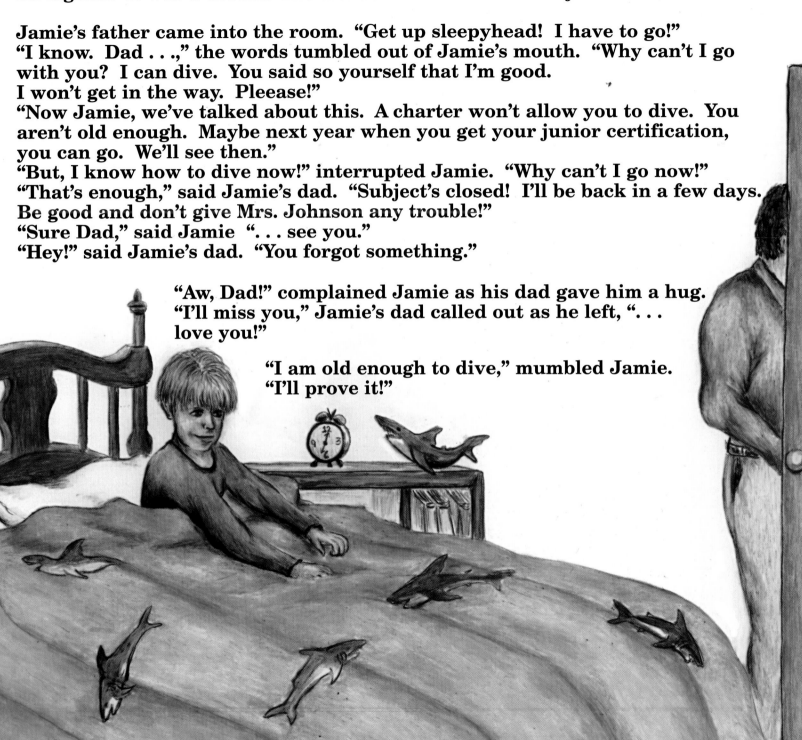

Jamie walked next door to Mrs. Johnson's house. Sam met him at the door. She was Jamie's best friend. Like Jamie, Sam had only one parent. Jamie didn't have a mom and Sam didn't have a dad.

"Hey, Mom just baked some cookies!" announced Sam. "C'mon, let's snag some!"
"Mom! Jamie's here!" called out Sam as she made a beeline for the cookies.
"Hello, Mrs. Johnson," greeted Jamie. "Something sure smells good!"
"Hi, Jamie," said Mrs. Johnson. "Help yourself!" "Thanks!" Jamie took several.
"Look what I have," said Sam, her mouth full, "a new shark book."
"Wow! Look at this Megamouth Shark!" exclaimed Jamie. ". . . and look at the Goblin Shark . . . Weird!"
"You certainly know a lot about sharks," commented Mrs. Johnson.
"Sharks are my life," answered Jamie seriously.
"Let's go in my room," said Sam, grabbing a handfull of cookies.
"Kids!" laughed Mrs. Johnson.

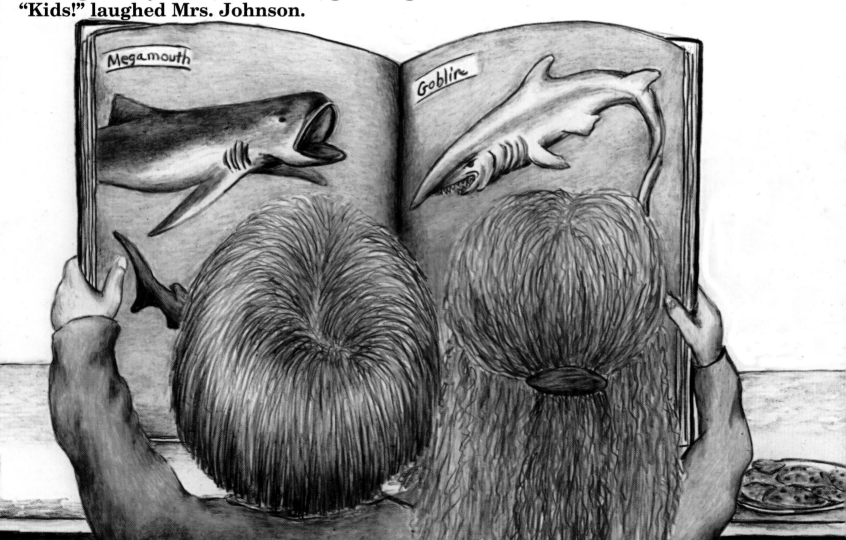

"I have something important to tell you," whispered Jamie, "but you have to promise not to tell anyone!"

"I promise," said Sam. "What is it?"

"I'm going diving!" Jamie confided. "I'm going to dive where there are sharks."

"But, you can't!" cried Sam. "It could be dangerous! You aren't certified and . . . well . . . you just can't that's all!"

"You sound like my dad!" complained Jamie. "I'm a good diver. I can do it!"

"I know you're good but . . .," said Sam doubtfully.

"I'm going. My mind's made up!" cried Jamie. "You can't talk me out of it!"

"Okay, if your mind's made up," said Sam. "But, I'm going too. You never dive without a buddy!"

"Thanks, Sam," said Jamie. "We'll go first thing in the morning. Right Buddy?"

"Right . . . sure," Sam agreed, then added under her breath, "I guess."

The next morning, Jamie and Sam were up before the sun. They ate a quick breakfast. Sam packed some sandwiches and snacks. Just as they were about to leave, Sam's mother came into the kitchen.
"Where are you two going so early?" yawned Mrs. Johnson. "It's only six . . . and what's all that?"
"It's our lunch," answered Sam. "We're going on a picnic."

"Yep, we're going on a picnic!" echoed Jamie.
"You better not be up to something!" warned Mrs. Johnson.
"We're just going to the marina . . . and have a picnic," said Sam.
"Then we're just going to do . . . you know . . . stuff!"
"Yeah, stuff . . .," agreed Jamie.
"Well, you better not get into any trouble," scolded Mrs. Johnson.

"And you had better be back here by supper. Understand!"
"Yes, ma'am," cried Jamie and Sam at the same time.

Jamie and Sam rode their bicycles to the marina. Jamie was going to take his dad's boat. "Are you sure about this?" asked Sam. "I mean diving with sharks . . . I don't know!" "Don't chicken out on me now!" said Jamie. "Besides, sharks hardly ever attack people. You have a better chance of getting struck by lightning than being bitten by a shark! Let's get the scuba gear ready! I know Dad has some full air tanks around here somewhere . . . ."

Sam struggled with her gear. A man looked up from the boat beside them and waved. It was Mr. Jones, a friend of Jamie's dad. Mr. Jones looked thoughtful, then he spoke, "Need some help with that stuff?" "Yes!" cried Sam. The man hopped onto the boat. "Looks like you're getting ready to dive," he said turning to Jamie. "Isn't your dad going? I don't see him."

"He's out of town," piped Sam. "We're going by ourselves!" Jamie shot Sam a look. "I see . . .," said Mr. Jones. "Well, let me give you a hand with this equipment."

"Is diving your job like Jamie's dad?" asked Sam. "No, not exactly, but I dive a lot in my line of work," answered Mr. Jones. "I study sharks."
"Oh, wow!" cried Sam, "Jamie just loves sharks! He's an expert. Jamie says sharks are his life!"
Jamie's face turned red. "I don't know everything . . .
I mean . . . I do read a lot!"
"I understand," said Mr. Jones. "Sharks are my passion too!"

"Tell us about sharks and stuff!" begged Sam.

"Well," began Mr. Jones, "I study sharks by finding out where they live, how many sharks are in an area, where they travel, how big they grow, what they eat, how many pups or baby sharks there are . . . things like that."
"How do you do all that? asked Sam.
"One of the main ways to get information is to tag the sharks," explained Mr. Jones. "We catch sharks and put tags on them. The tag doesn't hurt the shark. Then the next time we see or catch the shark, we can learn where it has gone, if it has grown, and other important information. We can even tag the shark with a transmitter and follow the shark as it moves through the water!"
"What other types of things do you study about sharks?" asked Jamie.
"One type of shark study or research may some day help humans," explained Mr. Jones. "Sharks rarely have cancer. So scientists are studying what is about sharks that makes them able to fight diseases such as cancer so well. So sharks may help us find ways to fight cancer in people!"
"I might want to study sharks when I grow up," commented Sam.

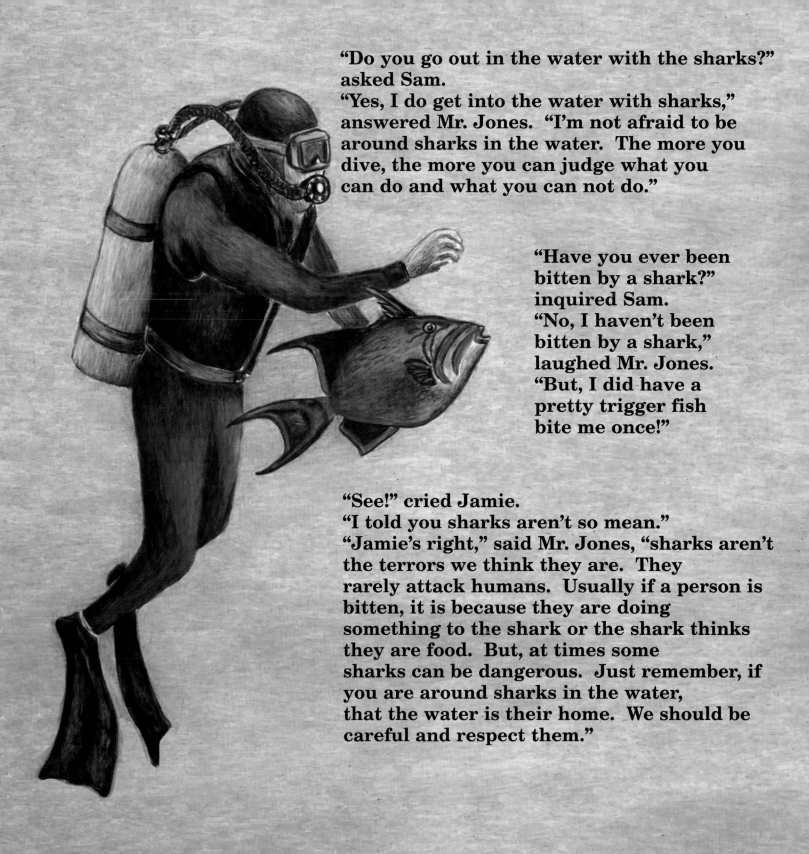

"Do you go out in the water with the sharks?" asked Sam.
"Yes, I do get into the water with sharks," answered Mr. Jones. "I'm not afraid to be around sharks in the water. The more you dive, the more you can judge what you can do and what you can not do."

"Have you ever been bitten by a shark?" inquired Sam.
"No, I haven't been bitten by a shark," laughed Mr. Jones. "But, I did have a pretty trigger fish bite me once!"

"See!" cried Jamie.
"I told you sharks aren't so mean."
"Jamie's right," said Mr. Jones, "sharks aren't the terrors we think they are. They rarely attack humans. Usually if a person is bitten, it is because they are doing something to the shark or the shark thinks they are food. But, at times some sharks can be dangerous. Just remember, if you are around sharks in the water, that the water is their home. We should be careful and respect them."

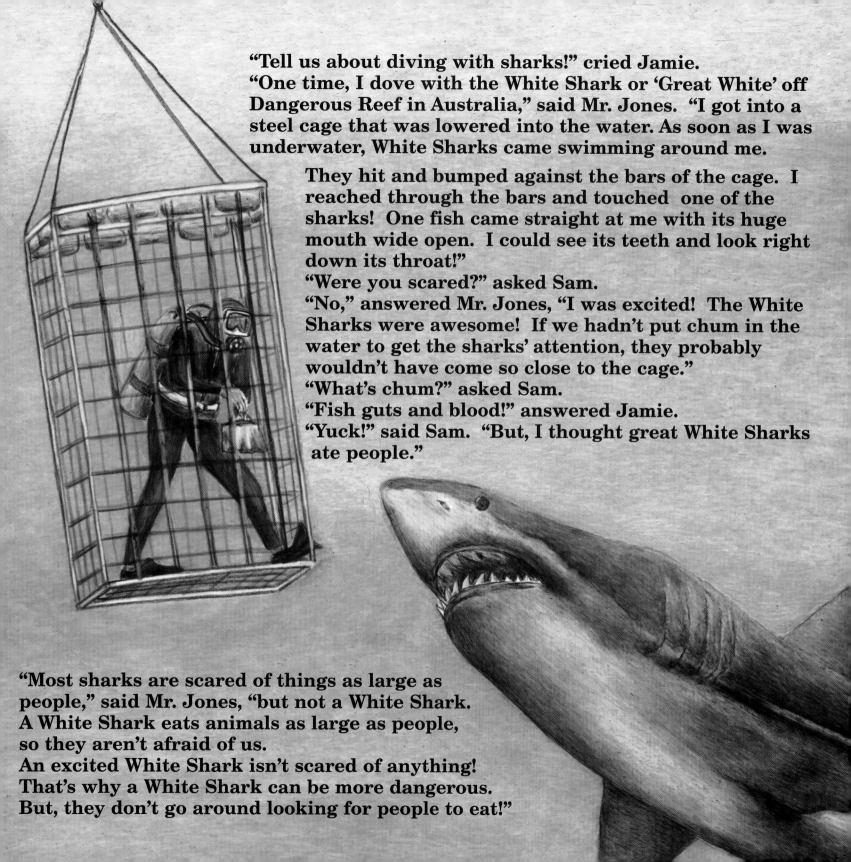

"Tell us about diving with sharks!" cried Jamie.
"One time, I dove with the White Shark or 'Great White' off Dangerous Reef in Australia," said Mr. Jones. "I got into a steel cage that was lowered into the water. As soon as I was underwater, White Sharks came swimming around me.

They hit and bumped against the bars of the cage. I reached through the bars and touched one of the sharks! One fish came straight at me with its huge mouth wide open. I could see its teeth and look right down its throat!"
"Were you scared?" asked Sam.
"No," answered Mr. Jones, "I was excited! The White Sharks were awesome! If we hadn't put chum in the water to get the sharks' attention, they probably wouldn't have come so close to the cage."
"What's chum?" asked Sam.
"Fish guts and blood!" answered Jamie.
"Yuck!" said Sam. "But, I thought great White Sharks ate people."

"Most sharks are scared of things as large as people," said Mr. Jones, "but not a White Shark. A White Shark eats animals as large as people, so they aren't afraid of us.
An excited White Shark isn't scared of anything! That's why a White Shark can be more dangerous. But, they don't go around looking for people to eat!"

"Sharks still scare me a little bit," confessed Sam.

"You scare sharks too!" said Mr. Jones. "A whole lot more people eat sharks than sharks eat people. Fishermen kill them for their fins. Sharks become tangled in nets and drown. People kill so many sharks that some kinds are dying out. If we don't protect them, there won't be any left!"

"My dad says if we knew more about sharks, we wouldn't be so afraid of them," added Jamie.

"That's right," continued Mr. Jones. "We must understand that sharks are in more danger from us than we are from them. We are the real 'terrors of the deep.'"

"I didn't know that," said Sam. "I don't want the sharks to die out!"

"We have to be responsible. We must realize that sharks are a small danger to people. We don't have the right to kill thousands of sharks because a few people have been attacked. We have to know our limits and the sharks' limits. Right Jamie!" said Mr. Jones. "As a diver, you should know about being responsible. A good diver knows his limits."

"Right!" agreed Jamie.

"I'll be going now," said Mr. Jones. "I guess you want to get started on that diving trip, huh?"

"We've changed our minds," answered Jamie. "We aren't really old enough or know enough to go diving by ourselves yet. To be honest, we haven't really dived except in shallow water with Dad around."

"That's a smart choice you made," said Mr. Jones. "When the time comes, I think you will make a great diver!"

"What a relief!" sighed Sam.

"Thanks for everything, Mr. Jones," said Jamie.

"Thanks," echoed Sam. "I liked hearing about sharks. I think they are neat too!"

"My pleasure," replied Mr. Jones, looking at his watch. "Look at the time! I've got to be going! Say 'hello' to your dad for me!"

Jamie and Sam ate their lunch
and started back to Sam's house.
"Are you going to tell your dad
about almost going diving?"
asked Sam.
"I have to. I mean . . . it's the right
thing to do," sighed Jamie. "He's
going to be mad!"
"I guess I have to tell Mom, too.
She'll kill me!" moaned Sam.
"I guess the only sharks I'll be
seeing any time soon will be in an
aquarium!" cried Jamie.
"Hey, Jamie look at me!" yelled
Sam, making a very goofy face.
"What was that?" laughed Jamie.
"I'm a scary terror of the deep!"
replied Sam.
"What a nut!" cried Jamie.
"Race you!"

*Shark Fin*formation

All sharks are fish. These super fish have lived in the world's waters for millions of years. There were sharks before there were dinosaurs! The huge Carcharodon Megalodon was a prehistoric shark. The Megalodon was probably the largest shark that ever lived. It may have been 43 feet long with five inch teeth. The White Shark or "Great White" as it's commonly called, is a close relative to the Megalodon.

There are over 300 different kinds of sharks. Some sharks are as big as a bus like the 45 foot Whale Shark, and some are tiny like the 12 inch long black Dogfish Shark. Many sharks are beautiful like the Blue Shark and the Mako Shark. Some are funny-looking like the Hammerhead Shark or the Goblin Shark. Some are unusual like the rare Megamouth Shark and the Cookie Cutter Shark.

Sharks have backbones made of cartilage. They have sandpaper-like skin covered with tiny sharp teeth called derma denticles. Sharks breathe by using their gills to get oxygen from the water. As the shark swims, water is drawn over and expelled through the gills. Most sharks can't pump water past their gills, so they must swim constantly so they can breathe!

A shark is a fast swimmer. Some sharks can swim up to 40 miles an hour! A shark glides through the water using its tail. It has dorsal and pelvic fins that guide it and keep it upright. Its pectoral or longside fins let the shark move up and down. A shark changes direction by bending its body. A shark cannot swim backward or stop very quickly.

Most sharks have sharp teeth to eat with. When a shark bites, it pokes out its lower jaw, draws back its snout, and snaps with its teeth. (A shark doesn't have to roll over to bite.) A shark grows back any teeth it loses. Most sharks eat other fish or animals. But some sharks, like the Whale Shark and the Basking Shark, eat plankton. The Whale and Basking sharks, though huge, have small teeth that they use to strain the plankton from the water.

Sharks aren't as scary as most people think. They are not the "terrors of the deep" that movies and books lead us to believe. Sharks rarely attack people — you have more of a chance of dying from lightning striking you than from a shark attack! Sharks are not stupid — they are the smartest of all fish. Sharks have even been trained to come for food when they hear a buzzer!

Sharks are amazing, wonderful creatures. They are well adapted to their watery home. Sharks are strong and healthy. (Sharks rarely get sick or diseased.) Sharks have few enemies. The only real threat to sharks is people! People have killed sharks for food, for their fins, or out of fear. Our man-made pollution and our trash kill sharks and other animals of the ocean. Some types of sharks are decreasing in number. We must study sharks and learn about them. Only when we begin to understand sharks will our fear of them fade. We must protect this unique form of life. Sharks, like every living thing, have their rightful place on this earth.

Denticles and other definitions

Ampullae of Lorenzini: jelly-filled sacs on the bottom of a shark's snout that senses the electricity that is given off by all living creatures. A shark uses them to find its prey.

Cartilage: tough, elastic animal tissue. (The stuff your ears and the tip of your nose are made of.)

Denticles: tiny, sharp teeth-like projections that cover the skin of a shark.

Dorsal fin: tall fin on a shark's back that keeps it from rolling.

Fins: organs used in swimming, balancing, and turning. (They look a little like airplane wings.)

Gills: organ used for breathing in animals that live in the water. (Sharks have gills.)

Pectoral fin: side fins that move the shark up and down.

Shark _Bytes_: Suggested Web Sites

Sharks
This site is one of my favorites! It is for grades K-3 and has many things to explore. Shark Facts, Animal Bytes and more! **http://www.siec.k12.in.us/-west/proj/animals/sharks.htm**

Fiona's Shark Mania
Has Images, info, and many links to other cool sites. **http://www.oceanstar.com/shark/**

Zoo and Aquarium Web Links
Click on to aquarium sites — has a shark site. **http://www.search-beat.com/zoo.htm**

For Parents, Teachers, and Kids: Check out Mote Marine Laboratory's site! Find some cool shark myths
at: **http://www.marinelab.sarasota.fl.us/-rhueter/sharks/mythm.phtml**
also for more info: **http://www.mote.org** _Teachers:_ Find out about Mote's Distance Learning at: **http://www.mote.org/-kristen/distance.phtml**

Shark Facts: Did you know? . . .

Some sharks such as Bull Sharks can live in fresh water! . . . The "Great White" Shark's correct name is just White Shark! . . . Sharks rarely attack people. You have more chance of dying from a bee sting than dying from a shark attack! . . . Skates and rays are close relatives to sharks! . . . Scientists are studying sharks and their ability to fight disease to help find ways to help humans with diseases such as cancer! . . . Sharks can drown or suffocate! . . . Sharks see very well! . . . Shark babies are called pups!